My Purple Umbrella

As a girl, I was able to be "boyish" and "girlish" without much, if any, harassment. I could play sports, wear shorts with a baseball hat, climb trees and build tree forts; then dress my cat up in doll clothes and take him for a stroll in my baby carriage around the block. After playing all day I could put on my Sunday best and people would compliment me on how diverse I was, telling me I could be anything I wanted to be. Society allowed me (and still allows me) to be extremely feminine, smart, athletic, and successful with the dream of breaking the glass ceiling. The message was clear...I could be ANYTHING a man could be. Yet, my son cannot live with the same freedoms.

There is such a visceral reaction to a man or boy being "too feminine". My son, Morgan, loves things that are pretty, sparkling, and flowing. The things that bring him joy fill his father's and my lives with immeasurable happiness. Morgan also has qualities society wishes for all children: he is empathetic, compassionate, thoughtful, respectful, caring and authentic.

I strive to live up to his level of authenticity. But after finding no local resources for our family, I decided to take action by creating My Purple Umbrella (MPU). MPU is a community where children can be free to express their gender expression and identity freely without judgment; they can build self-esteem, develop character qualities, and learn conflict resolution. Children thrive when having a sense of belonging that MPU provides.

The mission of "My Purple Umbrella" is to use play to provide a fun, loving, safe, and creative environment for gender independent children 13 and under. MPU also provides a support network for their families and caretakers. MPU kids "PLAY FREE!"

Lisa Keating, Founder and Executive Director, My Purple Umbrella

www.mypurpleumbrella.org + maxnmestudio.com = love

Max is 10. He's autistic. I'm McNall, his mom. Together we create kids' books to raise money for charities.

It might seem odd that an autistic kid and his mom would tackle a social issue like gender variance. That is unless you know the people we know and embrace their struggles as equally important. At the heart of everyone is a single truth: we all want to be accepted. Unfortunately, sometimes when we're true to ourselves, other people struggle to accept us. The lack of acceptance is difficult to grasp, and for Max, it's just not logical.

This book changed us in powerful ways. Meeting and becoming friends with Morgan, allowed Max to experience and express empathy toward his new friend. Meeting Lisa changed my life. Her desire to change the world so Morgan can be himself is the same powerful place that drives me to write kids' books with Max as a way to teach him about the neuro-typical world. As mothers, Lisa and I have totally different issues making life more challenging. But when you peel back that last layer of who and why we are... you find unconditional love is ultimately what's driving us. Writing this book in collaboration with Morgan, Lisa, Dmitri, Max and my life partner, Sue is an honor and a tribute to love and acceptance.

play free

written and illustrated by:

mcnall mason

and

max suarez

www.maxnmestudio.com

ISBN 978-0-9887499-2-4
published by MaxNmeStudio.com
Tacoma, WA

Dedicated To:

Morgan
&
Soozie

it's the place where
baby rainbows grow

until they let
their colors show

of wild adventures all around

of SUPERHERO capes

and dancing in gowns

it's a maGiCaL pLaCe to be
when You'rE someone who
looks as interesting as me

what's so **interesting**

a**bou**t me you s**a**y?

i think it's the way
i like to play

or maybe it's that
my hair is brown
or that i love to wear
my sparkly crown

but then it might be
my freckly left cheek
or that i like wearing
dresses a few times a week

honestly i'm not really sure why people think

i'm interesting or different while wearing some pink

don't get me wrong i know that i'm smart and good at ballet and make awesome art

so in case you'r₁ on₁ of
those who care
come a li^{tt}le closer
grab a chair
'cuz i have a li^{tt}le
story to share

really it'll only take
a minute or two

while i tell you about
this girl named sue

and when i am done
i bet you'll agree

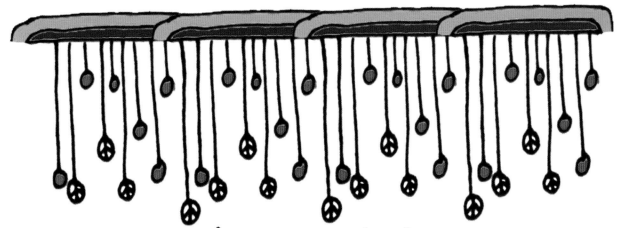

that she's kind of like you
and also like me

sue likes to play
with monster trucks
and go to
the park
to feed
the ducks

and sue wears what she wants
which isn't big news

'cuz girls can wear
pants and nobody boos

so was i right?
Can you see?

how you and sue are
similar to me?

Please take a minute
and have a good think...
have you ever considered
wearing some pink?

and **tell** me why
do PEOPLE stare

or ask me Questions
or even Care

about why it is
i wear a skirt

while playing with trucks
in piles of dirt

does it matter if
i LOVE flowery shoes
and all of THE colors
no matter their hues?

or read a book
or play with a toy

that some might think
is weird for a boy?

now that you see
and know it's true
that i'm like me
and also like you

we Can be MaRtians Wearing aliEn suits

or build a magical
flying igloo
and paint it pink
and purple and blue

so in the End
here's how this goes...
it's not about our
Choice of Clothes

it's really about saying
"i'm happy to be me"
while celebrating what it means
for us all to be free

and **that's how**

magic friendships start